Dolphin Heat Tamed

RONNIE F STRONG

written and published
by
Ronnie F Strong
Reservoir 3073, Victoria, Australia

ISBN 978-0-9943366-7-5

ronniestrong.com

licensed images used with permission
cover image: Yellowj, Yay images

Ronnie Strong is an author and publisher
of fine erotic stories and haiku.
His published works include:
Kate Gets Marks,
The Laundromat, and
Sex and other truths.

foreword

This story started a while ago on a holiday of mine. The place and experience stayed with me. I had dreams of dolphins. Nothing I could remember afterwards, except for them being beautiful and vivid. The dreams faded, but the idea for a story lived on.

When I later wrote my first *Dolphin heat* story, I exaggerated upon those dreams. I made the telling pure fantasy. Mainstream publishing sites blocked the books distribution. *Dolphin heat* contained descriptions deemed unacceptable for a general audience. I made the book available anyway and it is my most read, with many thousands of downloads.

I have revisited the *Dolphin heat* story, so it can enjoy a wider audience. Here it is: a tad tamed; though still a wild ride. I have endeavoured to make sure I lost none of the original spirit of the story. Focusing on the women's journey makes it better than before. I have added other elements to this book too, in keeping with the story's theme of exploration.

To complement the story, I have included some of my haiku on the *Dolphin heat* theme. They were all published on my ronniestrong.com website. The haiku are some of my readers' and own favourites. I reworked some of these too. I hope they provoke some further thoughts and feelings for you.

I invite you to treat this story as a whimsical saga. Life lived well is such a journey. We need to be open to all its possibilities, as we ontinue to work out our own boundaries and preferences. Before you start, a reminder. This is a work of erotic fiction.

My own standard for erotica is enjoyable explicit writing about sex and sexuality. It encourages reflection upon the main characters actions, qualities, quandaries and values. Erotica engages the reader in ways that give them pleasure on several levels. I hope you find all this in *Dolphin heat tamed*.

Ronnie F Strong
10 June 2018

rising beneath me
you find a snug warm welcome
which swallows you whole

The road was hot. The sand was hotter! Everything baked except for the air, steaming thick and heavy. Three days like this now and people were cranky and tired. Not me! I had never been so horny.

Last night's sex with Michael was great. As soon as he arrived at my little apartment I was kissing him and telling him to fuck me. I dragged him to my bed, pushing him down.

Ripping off his shorts, my shorts, and climbing onto him took thirty seconds. Before he had had a chance to say a word I was fucking him, needing him to please me right.

I pinned his arms up above his head and let my weight press down on him. That kept him still. He mewled and jerked underneath me. I would not let him touch my breasts. He strained his head up to reach. I leaned forward to let them tease his lips and tongue. I pulled away again before his teeth closed, jiggling and squirming.

Michael howled He wanted to rush and bang away. That was not allowed. I was in control and this was only the beginning. I wanted to fuck him slow in the way that got me hotter and hotter. He could wait for me this time.

Feeling selfish, I pressed more of my body weight down on his thighs and shoulders to hold him still under me. I shifted back on my knees, finding the perfect angle.

To help things along I steadied myself against his shoulder with my left arm. Then I reached down with my other hand. I parted and rubbed in fast little circles with my thumb; his prick sliding in and out between my fingers.

I could only stay like that for a minute or so before I had to use both hanfds to push Michael down again. He had a great body, which pleased me no end, but I was not going to let him change positions for a while yet.

A good five minutes of this had me shuddering and moaning. I released my hold to let him feel and bite my breasts and neck. Unable to stand it any longer, I swung around, pleading with him to fuck me from behind. I could not stop smiling in the wardrobe's mirrors as I watched him going for his life behind me.

released from darkness
fierce black desires of the void
overcoming you

My face shifted between half-snarls and wide grins. I looked further up at Michael standing above and behind me. His eyes glazed as he grunted and gasped. Neither of us could speak.

My whole body shook. Now Michael grunted and howled fuck, fuck, fuck, as he thrust, thrust, thrust. His yelling pushed me all the way there. We collapsed upon the bed, shaking and jerking. His thick cum foaming with my own fluids streamed out of me in spurts, mimicking his ejaculation.

All I had needed after that was a cold shower. The night was too hot to sleep snuggled against Michael, so I sent him home. Completely spent too, he did not argue. Some nights we fucked until the wet patch stretched from side to side right across the bed. Last night I was not so insatiable and fell asleep straightaway.

It might have been the relentless heat that made my dreams so vivid. I lay in bed trying to wake up, puzzling over these weird fantastical dreams. I soon forgot them, smiling at last night's amazing sex. These memories could keep me in bed for a bit longer. There was still time to amuse myself before I got up to leave for work at my family's boat-cruise business.

Business was good. My mother and father were flat out every day taking the boats on the cruises up the river and out to see the whales. I helped in the office, taking bookings from the holidaying tourists. Most of the customers were families with children. Sometimes the dads and mums were cute and flirty. Then I could have a little fantasy as we worked out the details.

I always got noticed by the men, happily-married dads included. I was not too flashy. I liked simple nice tight jeans or shorts and top to show my figure. I smiled for them as filthy thoughts ran through my smutty mind.

I especially liked it when pretty women noticed me. Attempting to explore this growing bi-curiosity of mine had not been too successful. A couple of times on a night out I had kissed and fondled girls in the same drunken condition as me. Things had not gone any further than that, so far.

experience shows
you do learn your boundaries
from overstepping

I hoped that one day a nice beautiful woman would seduce me. All she would need do is ask me to make love with her. Then she could take me home and caress and explore me in all the ways I so wanted. The thought of tasting a lovely woman's honey drove me wild. Despite that, I was not confident enough to proposition a woman. Even coming on to a man I fancied was beyond me, except for Michael. He was different.

At school I had been plain and bookish, full of big words and clever ways of saying things. Even worse, I was more used to two-way radios than texting or chats with my phone. My ways did not make me popular with either girls or boys during my teenage years. Being a nerd did mean I had lots of time for reading and fantasising. It also meant spending lots of time with my one close friend of either sex, Michael. He was my real-life boy-next-door and I was no longer a shy and uncertain schoolgirl.

Apart from being with Michael, I still found the whole sex and relationships thing hard. My body and the books I read gave me the ideas; but getting to know people my own age was more difficult. Having to do small-talk seemed like a minefield to me.

I found it easier to talk about stuff and what I wanted if I was a little typsy after a few drinks. The trouble was I did not like losing control. I found myself torn between wanting to let go while fearing letting go.

Luckily for me, and Michael too, we had added benefits to our close friendship. He satisfied my body's desires, without me having to worry about how I appeared to someone I did not know.

It was a bit confusing, but I figured I would work this stuff out, without having to hurry. After all I was still young and in the meanwhile I could please myself with Michael.

Thinking like this again about making love with a woman made me wonder if I should talk to Michael about it. He might have another girlfriend who could join us for a threesome. This stray thought magnified the sensations I was giving myself.

will I take the chance?
me my own worst enemy
playing innocent

An amazing amount of fluid poured from me, making my thighs glisten. I laughed, wondering why this idea had not occurred to me before. Michael would be up for it for sure, but first things first. I had to get ready for work, and spend another long day sitting around our jetty office in the stifling heat.

After that start to my morning, I allowed myself a languid breakfast, not rushing. After a long shower I got into my most fetching white cotton bra and panties. I was in that kind of mood and I looked dead-set sexy. I would have preferred skimpy black lace, but that was not practical for today's sweltering heat. Then I got into the skimpiest pure-white shorts and singlet top that I could get away with as my father and mother's employee.

Within minutes of beginning walking, I was sweating from the unusually high humidity. For a Saturday morning, there were few people around as I made my way to the jetty. Those who were out and about in the relative cool of the twenty-eight-degree morning wanted to get things done before the heat of the day kicked in. Most people were avoiding venturing out. They remained inside, hiding from the heat in their air-conditioned apartments, homes and shops.

There was no one waiting at our boathouse office when I got there. My father would have taken out a few keen anglers at dawn. They would be back soon, complaining the fish were not biting.

It would not worry me if we had hardly any customers for our boat cruises today. Whale and dolphin watching had given us good business over recent years. Our seven boats were heavily booked most days. A slow day or two would not be cause for panic. Maybe my parents could relax a bit and avoid the heat too.

As I opened the office a stunning woman appeared on the promenade. She slowed, waiting for me to make my way inside. I could only take in a little of her appearance as I fussed with the locks. What I could see of her had me flustered and fumbling. She cooed to me in a melodic gentle voice. "Don't rush honey; I can wait until you are ready for business."

looking you over
see you seeing all of me
and tremble, in awe

Something about the way she said that, with a hint of playful impishness, got me extra hot and bothered. Her clothing was much like mine, her mature and lovely body more graceful and full. Quite the bombshell, her body was not conventional pin-up.

She looked like a woman-shaped torpedo with her powerful sleek curves. Her legs were long and strong, bulging with muscle. Her neck was long too, not thick, yet somehow the torpedo impression remained with me. I kept glancing at her as I switched on lights, checked the radio, and did the other daily opening routines.

She wore no cosmetics or jewellery and her feet were bare. Her singlet top highlighted her full round breasts under the thin straps across the bodice. Her skin was glistening golden, not brown or white. Micro shorts showed off her tight butt and powerful legs. Her muscular thighs were larger than for most women. They complemented her statuesque body.

Short dripping-wet black hair framed her angular, almost squarish face. She did not need makeup. Her full lips and cheeks, grey-green eyes, black hair and perfect skin were stunning enough. What made her one of the most beautiful women I had ever seen was her nose. How it set off her face. It was largish, blunt and round, with flaring nostrils. Something else too, other than the mischievous glint in her eye had me entranced.

The way she held herself and shone with a glowing intensity was enthralling. I could not take my eyes away and tried to take in everything about her, helped by her skimpy clothes. The suggestion of a small circle low on her throat took my eye. It looked to me like she may have had a tracheotomy at some point. Could she have choked on something as a child, or had some kind of accident? I pondered this blemish upon her otherwise outward perfection, completely besotted. I forced myself to stop staring at her.

Uncomfortable prickling sensations were breaking out all over my body. Being in her company had me shrinking back to a nervous, gawky and insecure teenager. I thought I had shed all that awkward self-consciousness. Now all my self-doubts were back again.

take me to the place
where the dolphins throng and leap
to join them in play

I got past her somehow and went behind the desk, using it as a shield from her overwhelming impact upon my senses. She waited for me to collect myself then spoke, cooing like before.

"Could you please take me up the river to see the dolphins? I can pay whatever you need to charge for a special trip on one of your boats." Her voice was gentle and vibrant; the sound and energy of her voice touching me right to my core. My vagina swelled open with raw carnal desire. Wetness started oozing there, threatening to run down my thighs. My nipples pushed against my flimsy top. They were ruby hard, pointing out erect from my swelling breasts. The tip of my clitoris bulged, the heat of its engorgement stirring deep within the lowest part of my belly.

My body's quick and abundant reaction to her presence and request was beyond unsettling. For a moment I froze, not saying or doing anything as I fought with lust for control over my response. A moment went by as I waited for sensible words to return to me. She smiled, aware of her strong affect upon me and withdrew a step backwards. Then I could avert my eyes, breathe again, and try to think of something appropriate to say.

"I can take you," I finally blurted out. "We only have the larger cruise boat ready this morning, which costs a bit more, actually a lot for one person to pay. I am sorry, but I will have to charge you four-hundred dollars for an hour-and-a-half trip up the river on her. Is that okay?"

I waited, amazed that I had got all this out, although it had come in a bit of a rush. I could deal with this I realised. All I had to do was be professional and treat it as another day at the office. For our family, this meant taking customers on our boats up the Hastings River. Or out the heads to the Port Macquarie coast.

She smiled at me again. Four-hundred-dollars appeared from somewhere about her person, which she then handed to me. As she did so she got close to me and I swooned at the scent of her. It was not the raw animal smell that I had half expected. Nor was it the perfumed boudoir scent I had more expected.

nothing more perfect
floating away from it all
worries left behind

To my nose, her closeness suggested nothing other than the familiar smell of the river itself. She must have already had a swim this hot morning. I again feared drooling or moaning with lust. As before, she stepped back to soften her impact on me. Now I could make the necessary preparations.

I was about to call dad on the radio to let him know the details. Something made me stop and I wrote out a brief note instead. Then I locked the office behind us. I was not worried any other customers might turn up. It was pretty evident that this would be our only chance of a hire this morning. Dad would be both surprised and glad to see me and the boat gone. We always tried to meet every customer demand, no matter how eccentric, as long as it was safe and paid our going rate.

Our larger boat was already tied up and fuelled, ready for a river-cruise booking in the evening. I did not usually take her out as she was for our bigger party hires. I liked the idea of being able to show our beautiful guest I could do this for her. Keeping my physical reactions in check would be the hard part.

I told her that the new canals and housing development had unsettled the river dolphins. The excavation of these large artificial watercourses had altered their ancient ancestral home. Developers had built huge mansions on most of the new piles of mud. With the heat of this extended hot-spell I was not convinced we would find any dolphins. I explained we could cruise up the river and poke around the canals a little.

I hoped we might spot some dolphins, but I could not give any guarantees. She nodded agreement and bound up the gangplank onto Daphne.

The still conditions, in the thick humidity made casting off straightforward enough. The powerful outboards roared with the first kick of their starters. The throbbing of the engines settled me. In a moment we were creeping through the restricted speed zone. The slow rush of the river water past the keel calmed me more.

"What's your name? Mine's Dolly," she said.

beautiful woman
glorious and sensuous
got my attention

Her words, name and sweet voice bounced around inside my head for a moment. Confused, I realised I had not done any of the proper paperwork with her before setting off. She was patient. When I finally spoke, I relied upon some of our standard customer patter.

"I am Grace, and I am very pleased to meet you Dolly, and to welcome you aboard Daphne. She is our family's favourite boat for river cruising. We have to go slow here so that we don't cause wash, but I can open her up when we reach those markers ahead of us. There is bottled water in that ice chest, and you can sit anywhere you like. The life jackets are only needed in case of an emergency, I will make sure you have a safe and pleasant cruise up the ..."

I trailed off because Dolly — funny name for such a beautiful woman — had long stopped listening to me. She had made her way over to the ice-chest and was already draining most of an entire litre of cold bottled water.

To my surprise, she tipped the last third or so of the bottle down her front and over her bra-less breasts. Her top seemed to disappear highlighting her deep-brown nipples with their wide pink surrounds. Careless of her affect upon me, she quivered and shook, sending her nipples in exciting orbits. Her natural unaffected eroticism left me breathless.

Finished with the water bottle, she began exploring the boat. She strode full of energy, shining and glowing. She went to every quarter, like a super-model strutting the catwalk.

I told her what most passengers wanted to know. "The toilet is behind that blue door, at the rear of the cabin."

She looked at me blankly, and then continued her silent exploration on the deck.

Not knowing what else to do, I cranked up the throttle. We started motoring along at a gentle cruising speed of near ten knots. I noticed her first sign of hesitation as our speed increased. She stopped and looked at me, wondering.

you started something
came up to me and then roared
for satisfaction

"It's okay," I said, "I will keep my eyes out for dolphins, and I know this river backwards. We won't run into anything." I was proud of my ability to captain us on this little cruise, as straightforward as it was. She nodded satisfied, then went forward to stand at the bow.

There was no one else out on the river. We had it all to ourselves. No dolphins either, but I was not too surprised by that. She stood poised, keeping watch as we made our way upstream.

When we were about half a kilometre up the river she came up to me and told me she was taking her clothes off. I nodded okay, not certain about it at all. Without deliberate tease or display she pulled her shorts down and removed them. Her arms lifted, and her top dropped to the deck. Free of their imposition, she stood there naked. Graceful. Relaxing. her legs parted to steady herself against Daphne's gentle rocking. She had no hint of hair between her thighs.

I had to stand by the wheel. All I could do was feast upon her body with my eyes and mind, wanting to run my tongue over her. Especially between her thighs. She went out of the cabin, staying in my line of sight. Her legs parted wider as I watched. Her torso tilted forwards, pelvis backwards. She stretched, giving me even more of an eyeful of her loveliness. Was she now putting on an exhibition for me, knowing what I wanted?

Regardless of how I was feeling I had a job to do and so I kept the helm as we made our way in the climbing heat of the day. I was sure the temperature was already well over thirty degrees. The slight rush of wind from our movement through the water had no real cooling effect on me in the cabin.

I could not focus. The heat, humidity and the ache of wanting between my legs and deep in my belly drove me to distraction. Everything was going fuzzy. I had to concentrate on even the simple basics of navigation points. To my surprise, we were upon the first outlying houses of Settlement Point. I had not noticed us getting that far.

Dolly came in to the cabin. She tried out the seats and couches.

have me come rushing
when I hear you call my name
good to be wanted

Then she stood right next to me. That was good in one way.

"Does your boyfriend please you Grace?" The directness of her question surprised me. It was even harder to take in with her beautiful breasts right in front of me. They were ready for my hands and mouth. Despite the distraction, I was able to reply, impressing myself. "He is not a real boyfriend, but we do have a good understanding."

Some of my confidence was returning. Making love with Dolly was starting to feel like a real possibility. These thoughts were also a little terrifying, as I was not exactly sure what that might involve. I knew what I wanted to try and hoped that would be enough.

I was not sure if I could think straight and navigate the river when all I could think about was having sex with Dolly. It was so damned hot it was hard to think about anything at all. I tried to push the idea away but her suggestive presence next to me made that impossible.

"Grace, I want you to steer us to the end of the new canal, where they have not built houses yet. Can you do that?" I nodded. It was one of the common points we went to on our little river cruises. A solitary male dolphin was often there. He hardly ever left this stretch, except to venture out into the main channel for a quick bite to eat. She must have been thinking about him all along.

I was about to ask her about him when dad came on the radio, performing one of our standard checks to see if everything was okay. I looked at Dolly as I responded with our position and condition, which were unremarkable. I then turned the radio down, so we would not be disturbed again. She smiled, and I melted inside some more. For a few minutes she stood quietly next to me, helping me to get used to the feeling of her being close. Then she went aft to the ice-chest and downed another bottle of water. This time she drank every last mouthful. A little bead of water left her mouth, dripped down between her breasts, and then slid down her belly. It was the most erotic sight of my life. I trembled with lust, but still I hung onto the wheel and steered the boat.

burning with bright heat
soothe me, wash away the flames
quell this hot desire

Now finished, she shivered and shook, alerting me to something of her own inner condition. I dared to stare at her as she stood there. Her labia were an invitation, puffed and spread with excitement. Her vagina was open and ready with glistening wetness. My own condition matched hers.

I could not believe what I was seeing and feeling. I looked out at the heavy sky which pressed down on us with stifling heat and humidity. Sweat poured from my body making my cotton things damp and heavy. The sweat joined up between my legs with the moisture flowing there. My world narrowed in the curtain of thick heat and Dolly's presence. All that remained were the wheel in my hands and the dark line of the river ahead.

Dolly stalked around the cabin like a lioness on heat. Even in my confused state this comparison did not feel right. She was no stealthy feline. Her sleekness and playful smile was something else altogether. For a moment I contemplated her as a svelte muscular Labrador. That was not right either. Anyway, the looming passage of the ferry across our path meant I had to put any such further thoughts aside.

While my attention wandered, the Settlement Point ferry had begun its regular crossing. Only a truck or two, a few four-wheel drives, and a couple of cars were aboard her. Business was slow today for the large ferry too. She had right-of-way and I slowed the engines to an idle.

Dolly climbed up the forward stairs out of the cabin and onto the bow and walked right up to the railing. Her legs shifted a little and a torrent of piss streamed from between her legs. It splashed into the river more than a metre away from the hull.

I was both amazed and appalled. What would the good folk of Settlement Point make of the nonchalant naked pissing woman on our boat? Then I laughed so hard I was in danger of pissing myself, still standing at the wheel. It struck me what a waste that would be. Without another thought, I turned the rudder further away from the ferry's course.

letting it all go
under the hot summer sun
as I melt away

Letting Daphne drift in the wide bend for a moment would be safe. That done, I pulled off my sodden clothes and rushed onto the deck to stand beside Dolly. There I relieved myself, allowing my golden piss to mingle with hers in the brown water of the river. Release washed over me. From the hold of my clothes on my body, my tight holding of the wheel, and now from the holding of my bladder. The last vestiges of my usual self swept away in an intoxicating flowing rush.

Dolly had taken me to another world. With her there were different expectations, rules and ways of behaving. Finding myself in this different place elevated my horniness to a new level. Completely beside myself, I shook with the want possessing every single part of me. I was desperate to fuck and to fuck in every way imaginable.

My last dribbles of urine disappeared into the river as I shook and shivered. I gathered myself resisting the strong urge to throw myself at Dolly. Wantonness aside, someone still had to steer Daphne. I rushed back to the wheel, increased the throttle, and steered us back to the middle of the river channel.

We were past the ferry, which had now completed its short trip from the north to south bank. The vehicles were already driving off her as we made our way past. I expected jeers, blaring horns and lots of heckled crude advice. Instead, complete silence met our naked pissing performance off the side of the boat. It was as if it had never happened.

With that odd episode over, I needed to give some more serious attention to navigation. We had now made the Point and were close to the canal system entrance. I wanted to tuck us into the wide northern groin after making the entrance, past the bend.

The overpowering heat and humidity and my state of mind restricted my field of vision. I struggled to see anything beyond the water breaking around the bow. With only minutes of our journey left, I just needed to cope, despite my confusion.

My attention strayed to Dolly. How strange and lovely she was.

a river siren
calling. I dived down with her
drowning me in love

So unlike any other woman I had ever encountered. I again wondered what might happen when we got to her destination. Who was this curious woman really? Should I instead be asking what was she? What was she going to do there? There were plenty of clues to suggest something amazing would happen. For sure, it would be something beyond anything else in my experience.

I would not have to wait long to find out. Her whole body rippled as she strained to remain in control. She shimmered with the heat of the sexual energy and desire bursting from her. Aware of my gaze, she looked back at me with unabashed lust. Her wide playful eyes dwelt on every inch of my sweaty nude body assessing me for her purposes. She made beautiful little guttural sounds as she examined me. They were nothing like Michael's loud grunting of last night. These melodic noises were far from uncontrolled groans of passion. This was a song of hers directed at me.

The exotic refrains started making sense to me. Her song was not about romantic love or love lost. This song was an ode to lust and its satisfaction. It was a fucking song, a music and language of fucking. Her singing was a celebration of the body and all the holes and bumps at its leaky boundaries. There was to be a festival of the vagina, nipples, mouth, clitoris, anus and the penis. Her song was all about enjoying the body and sharing it with others. This song was part ritual, part seduction and foreplay!

I was already beside myself with lust before listening to Dolly's song. Now I had one hand on the wheel and one hand between my legs, hoping this might be enough for the moment. Dolly's self-control was stronger than mine. She moved aft, still singing, and leaned over the stern, giving me a most remarkable view.

She pushed her fingers through the water as she trilled and grunted. I lost myself in watching and listening to her.

I could hardly see the banks of the canal anymore. I somehow kept navigating without any conscious awareness of what I was doing.

searching for joy, peace
see how beauty surrounds us
all of creation

My horniness, the boat, the wheel, the heat, the humidity, the river and Dolly had become my entire world.

When she moved forward again I knew the next part of our journey was starting. I spotted the unmistakable movement of a large dolphin cutting through the water. This beautiful dolphin was leading our way. Behind us, there was a whole pod of dolphins playing and jumping as they followed our boat.

I was a little surprised by their magical appearance; but I was rapt for Dolly. I wanted her to see what she had come for.

She stood motionless for a moment watching them. She then turned towards me with her playful smile to call out. "Grace, have you ever watched dolphins having sex?" I had often seen them doing it and so I nodded yes, while working my way closer to give a proper answer. I decided that the safest thing was to simply say what I had seen them do.

"They look like they really enjoy it, but they don't seem able to do it for long. It seems pretty quick to me." I did not know what more to say and waited for her to say something else. She turned and stared up ahead again.

The dolphin she was looking at was a large male that my parents had often talked about over the last few months. He always appeared to be in this groin of the system. He spent all day going up and down, and around and around, as if trapped there, except he was not. This stretch was the last housing development. There were only the beginnings of some roads and foundations on the nearby banks.

We had passed through the established sections without me even noticing. Those parts had large houses and the people who lived in them on all sides. Both of us were stark naked. I could not understand how we had made it here at all, let alone without someone hailing or accosting us.

Some sort of protective spell had to be cloaking us from view. We were in our own little world of dolphins, heat, moisture, water and carnality. I killed the engines, letting us drift.

fancy swimming down
diving deep in the water
flowing so freely

The flow of air stilled. The moist heat came closer, blanketing my naked body in sweat. The gentle sloshing of our boat only heightened the sense of silence.

My thinking was all muddled and I had no real idea of what might happen next, although I had my suspicions. Regardless, I was still the mistress of our vessel and responsible for her safe condition.

I forced myself to focus on my next task, not wanting to interrupt this quiet sojourn of gliding motion. Dolly stood next to the anchor housing, knowing that I would be making my way there. I untied the chain, and then jumped a little at the sound of the anchor's large splash into the river. Dolly's physical presence somehow reassured me in all the strangeness that was pressing in on me. She gave me a wicked smile, and then leapt into the water in an arching dive. For a moment I did not know what to do, and then I followed with a less graceful belly-flop.

After everything else, plunging into the tepid water of the canal was calming. Underneath the surface everything was peaceful. I rose up and looked around. The dolphin school maintained a flowing circling perimeter around us and the boat. I thought the first male was still close, somewhere inside the moving circle.

I dived down again, staying under as long as I could. I swam around, getting used to the feeling of the water, and trying to locate Dolly or the male without much success. Holding onto the last of my breath, I half spied her through the brown opaque water. She skimmed at speed along the bottom of the canal, at home in a familiar environment.

Her grace was beautiful. Such supple and powerful movement through the flowing water. Reluctantly, I surfaced to let the hot air from above the water into my bursting lungs. I could not imagine how she managed to hold her breath for so long.

Unable to chase her, I treaded water; waiting for Dolly to come to me. I kicked my legs, sending them in lazy wide circling motions. My arms were pushing through the water to support me too.

I offer myself
let me move with your power
bring down love and joy

I looked down at my breasts bobbing in the water and for a long gorgeous moment I was beautiful and free. Dolly's intimate caress could be the only possible improvement.

I laughed as Dolly surfaced from beneath me. She forced her way up between my legs, brushing me there with her mouth and tongue. Little bubbles of air ran up my belly, accompanying her long rising kiss. She broke the surface, snatched a quick breath, and clamped her mouth to mine in a deep French kiss. Our breasts pressed together, our nipples hard. Her fingers were exploring deep inside me as we sunk beneath the water, locked together.

I kissed her back with everything I had, completely unafraid. I wrapped my legs around her upper thighs as she propelled us with rapid little thrusts of her feet. Her hold was strong and reassuring. Time stopped. My world shrunk to the feeling of our bodies pressed together.

Her long fingers inside my happy vagina was magnificent. We broke the surface, and she put another finger higher behind me. She had me suspended weightless upon her fingers inside me in two places. She never stopped kissing my breasts, neck, lips, eyes and face. I exploded into orgasm, gasping for air. Pleasure throbbed outwards from my lower belly, deep inside me. It was the release I had been waiting for since her arrival at the office.

I wanted to give her the same pleasure that she had given me. First, I needed to let my still quivering body settle and myself relax as she propelled us back to the boat's stern. After releasing me from our embrace she hauled herself into the boat. She then reached down to help me clamber aboard.

Without a word we were again pressed together in a loving intimate hug. We edged back into the cabin, collapsing together on the larger cabin divan. She laid back, opening herself to me, inviting me to please her. I lay my body over hers, then wrapped my legs around her. We kissed and kissed each other, exploring one another's mouth, neck and face with our lips and tongues. After a few minutes of this kissing and grinding, I shifted myself around.

*slow gentle caress
rises higher, toes to thigh
sinks in luscious depths*

I wanted to straddle her in a low crouch. Dripping and wide open, I then slowly glided myself up her belly and over her breasts. I gradually pushed myself upwards to her mouth, leaving a trace of my oozing wetness on her smooth golden skin. The mouth of my vagina and the tip of my clitoris were finally met by her lips and tongue. I came again with a loud shriek, unable to bear her flicking tongue. It was too much, having been swollen for what felt like hours.

As soon as I had stopped throbbing, I flipped myself around and knelt on the floor of the cabin, between her legs. I plunged my tongue deep within her vagina. I licked her everywhere from her tight hole between her divine buttocks, and up to her exquisite bud.

She was singing her song, as I licked and nuzzled, tasting the slight saltiness of her dripping fluids. I slowed down, not wanting to rush and licked around my fingers which I had pushed into her grateful vagina. I adjusted the angle of my hand, allowing me to push my thumb into her anus. Then I pushed my fingers together to feel them touching through the slippery walls. Her song changed to a shuddering moan and she came with a gush.

I stopped my deep touching and watched the mouth of her sweet vagina pulse open and close with pink delight. Seeing Dolly's intimate and amazing response to my touch gave me another rush of pleasure. She then thrashed around, not letting go of her own nipples, stretching and pinching them hard. I could do that too. I pulled her fingers away and locked my teeth around her right nipple. I bit hard and then sucked and nuzzled. I cradled as much of each of her superb breasts as I could manage.

She responded by pushing two or more fingers into my pleased vagina. She churned them around inside me, making me bite even harder on her captive nipple. Our love-making was even more exquisite than I could ever have imagined. I could go on like this for hours if Dolly was up for it. She was squealing into another shuddering orgasm, and then pulling away from me.

in my happy place
two bodies yearn, merge and flow
with a rising tide

I released my biting clamp upon her rock-hard nipple as I felt her moving. Freed, she jumped up and dived straight over the side of the boat. I touched myself where her fingers had been. Missing them. I wanted her to keep fucking me, but she had already gone without even a splash to mark her exit.

I wanted more of this glorious first-time sex with a woman. That meant joining her in the water again. Leaving the cabin, I tried spotting her from the bow.

Now I knew why she had come to my office today. I could not see Dolly any more. There were only dolphins in the water now. Two were frolicking together, only metres from the boat. They swam joined together for a short while and then parted. One did a quick little circle and they were together again. Once again, it only lasted a short time. One swapped its direction to face me with a happy dolphin face. The other one repeated his previous manoeuvre and was soon beside her again.

The squealing noises they were making sounded like Dolly's fucking song. Apart from this, and their splashing movements, the world was still and quiet. I was their spellbound witness in this shrunken heat and water-filled world. touching myself the whole time. It looked like they wanted me to watch them, but I may have been wrong.

The female sunk from view beneath the water. I took this as my cue and allowed myself to reach a little whimpering orgasm. I shook with pleasure. I looked out over the water to see the male dolphin watching me with complete understanding.

Something mystical was happening here. I had become a part of an exotic ceremony from another world altogether. I had only one concern for this intense life-changing encounter.

I feared I would not be able to really understand what was happening here. My excitement and mind-blowing physical pleasure was overshadowing any possibility of true communion.

My heart pumped loud in my ears. My mind filled with the buzz of whirling multiplying thoughts and fears.

your amazing touch
bringing me closer to the edge
where I come crashing

My turned-on body was different. It knew how to respond to all this intense stimulation. I focused on the warm stirrings deep in me. I would be okay. I looked around and saw Dolly beside me, in her human form again.

Now her vagina was streaming with thick white fluid. She gently pushed my head away as I tried to nuzzle her. She had other ideas and reached out her hand to help me up. "He is waiting for you," she said. I jumped over the side and treaded water like I had before when waiting for Dolly. I was not sure what I was meant to be doing.

As soon as I settled in the water his rushing body whooshed up the front of my body. His prick was inside me before I had time to gasp. It was so good all I wanted to do was swoon. I opened my eyes and saw a handsome man's face looking into mine. I wrapped my legs and arms around his strong body, while also squeezing his prick snug inside me.

He was treading water too, holding his station inside me, helped by my tight grip around his barrel of a body. Our heads were close together. His grey blue eyes looked straight into mine, mad with horniness.

I wanted to understand what was happening to me. It was hard to believe what I was doing, but I did not want it to stop. With everything going on, keeping hold off him in the water was difficult. After only seconds, we began to fall apart. I wanted more of that.

I sank under the surface as he slipped out of me. I watched him power away in a steep dive. His muscular body and agility were magnificent. This time he came up behind me. The surprise only made it even more perfect. With strength and balance, he somehow pushed his way into my tight rear. Amazed and liking it, I did my best to help steady us by pushing my arms backwards.

This gave him a bit of a guiding frame as he kicked upwards against me. The feeling of his prick pushing into me there for that moment was incredible. Now he swum past me on his back.

go on, take the bait
nibble my tasty morsels
and find yourself hooked

His crooked prick pointed and shook at me. I reached out and grabbed it with my hand and pulled on him up and down as he floated by. In shape and size, it was a lot like any other man's uncircumcised prick. As well as being crooked, it was pointier than Michael's. Seeing it had me thinking about another thing for me to try. I wanted to taste him. Luckily for me, he was turning towards me again, still on his back. I leapt across the water and onto him, taking his bent prick into my mouth. I sucked as hard as I could before we fell apart once more.

On my next chance, I was able to keep him in my mouth for longer. I gave him my hardest suck ever. His prick swelled and jerked in my mouth. I knew I was about to drink his thick cum.

Losing my battle to keep my nose above the water, we had to separate and try again. When he dived, I understood he had a different idea. I treaded water again, my legs spread wide in the hope that he might take me in that rushing climb again. Instead there was the hint of a feathery touch. Somehow, he was using his tongue to lick me. It only lasted a few seconds. This tender gesture brought me to the very edge of a shattering orgasm anyway.

The part of me keeping me afloat was getting concerned. With all the lust and pleasure going on in me it was hard to find my breath. I began to worry I would get so worked up that I would drown.

His next move pushed my fears away. He was inside me again, and somehow giving me a delicate rub there too with a free hand. I was swooning; convinced that I was going to die, either from drowning or intense pleasuring. The amazing sensation lasted longer as our bodies kept colliding together. I held my position in the water and let myself relax into this amazing and surprising fuck. He swung around and was tasting and touching me again.

Waves of pleasure washed through my body. I wanted his penis inside me again.It was time to feel his cum spurting inside me, splashing the walls of my vagina with great gobs of his thick cream. He must have been of the same mind.

heated body writhes
begging for your knowing touch
finish with a splash

He rushed up my front, his prick jerking away inside me once more. The black pupils of his eyes rolled up and disappeared upwards into his skull. Everything went dark, so my own eyes must have done the same, or they simply closed.

Feeling my way, I got a firm hold with my legs and arms wrapped tight around him. There was a sudden surging sensation of rapid acceleration. The weightlessness of falling followed. As we fell my vagina throbbed into a massive orgasm. I knew his penis was spurting his cum deep inside me too, as I had wanted.

His huge leap out of the water, with me held tight riding him, was finally ended by gravity. I had to close my mouth as water crashed over me.

I lost my hold around his body. Somehow his throbbing prick was still inside me, thrusting me along with him a little further. Finally, this remaining intimate grip released too.

I surfaced and waited, treading water, allowing my racing heart to calm. The whole experience was so dream like that I started to think myself invulnerable. The moving perimeter of the pod made me think they would keep me safe in their world.

Was I a sex goddess to these dolphins, or was I more like an offering? I did not care. What a rush this experience had been.

I was not sore at all, even though some of his attentions had been a little rough. I hoped there might still be some more. I looked around, I could not see Dolly again.

The moving parade of the dolphin pod had changed. One of the beautiful creatures had left the moving circle and was heading straight for me. I kept treading water and readied myself. This young male pushed against me and I patted him, not knowing what else to do. He fell away from me squealing as he left.

The next dolphin was already upon me and then another. A heaving mass of warm excited bodies rushed at me. They all wanted me to touch them.

Unrestrained sexual activity surrounded me. The members of the pod were having a full-scale orgy. This was way outside my experience or fantasies. It was eerily beautiful.

41

magic between us
there from our first gentle touch
soon a wild frenzy

The water churned with hyper-sexually-excited dolphins. I could not tell which were males and which were females. They were all at one another. This went on and on. At some point, I again worked out which one was Dolly, in her dolphin form. She swam up and nuzzled me. I was too tired to respond.

Confused thoughts and emotions washed over me. I was having real trouble staying afloat. I was done.

The dolphins were also getting tired. A different mood came over us and their wild orgy was over. The water stilled, and the dolphin pod resumed the moving perimeter around me.

I tried swimming towards the boat. I was spent. Not wanting to panic I rolled over on my back to float and rest for a moment. What had just happened to me and who was that man? At that exact moment he swam up to me and took me in a lifesaver hold, I smiled. Dolly was helping me too. Together they took me back to my boat with me resting between them nice and safe. Not expecting an answer, I tried asking him his name. I could not tell if he even heard me, I got no answer.

When we drew alongside the stern they pushed and helped me haul myself aboard. I collapsed upon the deck. I closed my eyes glad to be out of the water with a firm surface beneath me. I lay there for a moment wondering what I should do, completely unable to move. I heard someone climbing aboard.

Strong arms picked me up and carried me to the divan where I had lain with Dolly an eternity ago. Gentle hands lifted my head. Soft sweet lips kissed my mouth, and then a water bottle touched against my lips. I took a deep drink, still without opening my eyes, not wanting to break this last spell. A beautiful man's voice said a single strange-sounding word, which I could not recognise. I smiled, realising he had given me his name, even though I could not repeat it. I opened my eyes to thank him.

I was alone. I looked over the side all around and there was no trace of him, Dolly or the dolphins anywhere. The heat still pressed down on me.

I cried till I laughed
trying out those wicked things
we were outrageous

I shook myself, not sure of anything. I found my white things, all a little brown, and decided that I had to put them back on.

Before getting dressed I looked down to see if what I looked like matched with what I could feel. Could all those goings-on be real?

Well there was abundant evidence between my legs to confirm it was not my imagination. I was all flushed, scarlet and pink. Some river water dribbled from me too.

I shook again, this time in pleasure, with the memory of my last few hours. Now I panicked, realising I had planned on a short cruise when actually I must have been gone for hours.

My parents would soon be thinking about searching for their missing boat, and her crew and passenger. I pulled on my clothes, not worrying about my river-soaked body and the traces of sex all over me. Grabbing the radio mike, I sang out Daphne's call sign and asked for a response. Dad was straight back to me from the office radio. "Is it hot enough for you out on the river darling. What possessed you to take yourself out for a cruise on a day like today?" He did not sound concerned at all, only puzzled.

Not for the first time today I was speechless. I told him I was safe at anchor and that I had fallen asleep in the heat. Then I asked him what the time was. His answer confused me even more. I got off the radio, telling him I would head straight back.

I had to check first. There were a couple of empty drink bottles on the cabin floor near the ice chest. Did that prove anything?

As I motored back the thirty-minute journey, I kept wondering. How could I only have been gone not much more than an hour? I did not spot a single dolphin the whole way back, and the ferry stayed out of my way.

Wht had happened to me with Dolly and her dolphin friends? In the unrelenting heat and humidity, I shivered and laughed aloud.

you can have it all
swim in the ocean and sky
bask in air and sun

Images

www.ingramcontent.com/pod-product-compliance
Lightning Source LLC
Chambersburg PA
CBHW041033170626
46815CB00010B/21